The Grosset & Dunlap
Read Aloud Library

This book belongs to

Jessica Weintraub

With love from
Aunt Fern & Barrie
10/27/91

The Grosset & Dunlap Read Aloud Library

BEDTIME STORIES

Publishers • Grosset & Dunlap • New York

BEDTIME STORIES

Compiled and adapted by Dina Anastasio

Contributing Editors
Margo Lundell
Oscar Weigle

Illustrated by Lucinda McQueen

A member of The Putnam Publishing Group

To Jeremy
           —LM

Copyright © 1987 by Dina Anastasio
Illustrations copyright © 1987 by Lucinda McQueen.
All rights reserved.
Published by Grosset & Dunlap, a member of the Putnam Publishing Group, New York.
Published simultaneously in Canada.
Printed and bound in Singapore.
Library of Congress Catalog Card Number: 86-83305
ISBN: 0-448-10551-9
A B C D E F G H I J

Contents

Little Red Riding Hood

In a neat cottage standing by itself at the edge of a forest lived a little girl whose name was Little Red Riding Hood. It wasn't her *real* name, but people called her that because she always wore a bright red velvet cloak and hood that her grandmother had made for her.

One morning after breakfast Red Riding Hood's mother packed a lunch of good things to eat. She filled a basket with apples, oranges, grapes, gingerbread, cookies and jam. "These are for your grandmother, who isn't feeling very well," she told the little girl. "I want you to take this basket to her right away. Just stay on the path as you go through the woods to her house, then give Grandma a kiss for me and one for yourself, and come back as soon as ever you can."

Little Red Riding Hood was happy to visit her grandmother, since she loved her dearly, so she took the basket and set out. As she entered the forest, however, a wolf suddenly appeared on the path.

"Good morning, little girl," said the wolf in his gruff voice. "And where might you be going this fine day?"

Now the wolf was no friend, and Red Riding Hood should not have said a word. Instead she answered, "I'm bringing this basket of goodies to my sick Grandma who lives on the other side of the forest."

Well, that was all the wicked wolf had to know to make plans of his own. He would get to the grandmother's house before Little Red Riding Hood.

"See the pretty flowers growing all around us," said the wolf. "Why not pick some and take them to your grandmother as well?"

Red Riding Hood was sure that her grandmother would be pleased to have a pretty bouquet, so she picked some of the brightest flowers she could see. Meanwhile, the wolf slipped away behind the trees and took a shortcut to the grandmother's house.

And what should the wicked wolf do when he got there but gobble up the old woman, all in one piece! Then he quickly put on her nightclothes and jumped into bed, pretending to be the grandmother.

When Little Red Riding Hood arrived at her grandmother's house and went into the bedroom, she could hardly believe her eyes. "Grandma," she cried. "What big ears you have!"

"The better to hear you with, my dear," the wolf replied.

"Grandma, what big eyes you have!" said Little Red Riding Hood.

"The better to see you with, my dear," answered the wolf.

"And, Grandma, what big teeth you have!"

"The better to eat you with!" the wolf growled, leaping
out of bed. And before the little girl could say anything
more, she was swallowed in one greedy gulp.

With a doubly full stomach, the wicked wolf crawled back
into bed, closed his eyes, and was soon snoring loudly.

It so happened just at this time that a hunter was passing
by the house. When he heard the sound of loud snoring, he
decided to take a look inside. And when he saw the wolf fast

asleep in Grandmother's bed, he knew exactly what had happened. He took out his hunting knife and in a moment cut open the bulging stomach of the wicked wolf. In the very next moment Little Red Riding Hood sprang out.

The grandmother was quite safe, too, and was happy to see her grandchild. Then they all sat down to a picnic lunch, since there was enough food in the basket for all, and the flowers Red Riding Hood had picked surely did cheer up her grandmother.

Best of all, the forest was free of the wicked wolf, for which everyone felt most particularly thankful!

Goldilocks and the Three Bears

Once upon a time there were three bears who lived in a house in the woods. One was a great big Papa Bear, one was a middle-sized Mama Bear, and the last was a wee small Baby Bear.

One day, the bear family made porridge for breakfast. While the porridge cooled, the bears went for a walk in the woods. After they were gone, a little girl named Goldilocks came upon the bears' house. Being curious, she opened the door and went in.

Goldilocks was hungry, so she was happy to see three bowls full of porridge on the table.

First she tasted the porridge in the great big bowl, but it was too hot. Then she tried the porridge in the middle-sized bowl, but it was too cold. Then she tasted the porridge in the wee small bowl, and it was just right. Goldilocks liked the porridge so much that she ate every bit of it.

Goldilocks went to another room and saw three chairs. She tried to sit in the great big chair, but it was much too hard for her. Then she sat down in the middle-sized chair, but it was too soft. Finally she tried the wee small chair, and it was just right. But no sooner had she plopped herself down than the small chair broke all to pieces.

Goldilocks went upstairs and found a room with three beds in it. Feeling tired, she lay down on the great big bed, but the mattress was too hard for her. Next she tried the middle-sized bed, but it was much too soft. Finally Goldilocks lay down on the wee small bed, and it was just right. So she covered herself up and fell fast asleep.

By this time the three bears had come home to their breakfast. Papa Bear saw a spoon in his porridge bowl. "SOMEBODY HAS BEEN EATING MY PORRIDGE!" said Papa Bear in his great big voice.

Then Mama Bear saw a spoon in her bowl, too. "SOMEBODY HAS BEEN EATING *MY* PORRIDGE!" said Mama Bear in her middle-sized voice.

When Baby Bear saw his little bowl, he cried out in a wee small voice, "SOMEBODY HAS BEEN EATING *MY* PORRIDGE, AND HAS EATEN IT ALL UP!"

The three bears began to look around. Papa Bear saw that the hard cushion in his great big chair was not straight. "SOMEBODY HAS BEEN SITTING IN MY CHAIR!" he shouted in his great big voice.

Mama Bear saw that the soft cushion in her middle-sized chair was all rumpled. "SOMEBODY HAS BEEN SITTING IN *MY* CHAIR!" she exclaimed in her middle-sized voice.

When Baby Bear saw what had happened to his chair, he cried out in a wee small voice, "SOMEBODY HAS BEEN SITTING IN *MY* CHAIR, AND HAS BROKEN IT ALL TO PIECES!"

Then the three bears went upstairs to take a look. Papa Bear saw that someone had wrinkled the cover on his great big bed. "SOMEBODY HAS BEEN LYING IN MY BED!" Papa Bear boomed out in his great big voice.

Mama Bear saw that the cover on her bed was not straight. "SOMEBODY HAS BEEN LYING IN *MY* BED!" said Mama Bear in her middle-sized voice.

And when Baby Bear looked at his bed, there was Goldilocks, fast asleep. "SOMEBODY HAS BEEN LYING IN *MY* BED," cried Baby Bear in his wee small voice, "AND SHE'S STILL HERE!"

The squeaky voice of the wee small bear awakened
Goldilocks. When she saw the three bears looking down at
her, she jumped out of bed, raced down the stairs, and ran
out of the house as fast as she could.

Since Goldilocks never returned, the three bears never saw
the little girl again.

18

The Little Red Hen

Once upon a time there was a Little Red Hen who found some grains of wheat.

"Who will help me plant this wheat?" the Little Red Hen asked the other animals in the barnyard.

"Not I," growled the Dog.

"Not I," meowed the Cat.

"Not I," grunted the Pig.

"Then I will plant this wheat all by myself," clucked the Little Red Hen.

She planted the wheat, and before long it grew tall and yellow.

"Who will help me cut and thresh the wheat?" the Little Red Hen asked the animals in the barnyard.

"Not I," growled the Dog.

"Not I," meowed the Cat.

"Not I," grunted the Pig.

"Then I will cut and thresh the wheat all by myself," clucked the Little Red Hen.

The Little Red Hen cut the wheat and threshed it and gathered it all up in a sack.

Then she spoke to her friends again. "Who will help me take the wheat to the mill?" asked the Little Red Hen.

"Not I," growled the Dog.

"Not I," meowed the Cat.

"Not I," grunted the Pig.

"Then I will take the wheat to the mill all by myself," clucked the Little Red Hen.

She carried the sack all the way to the mill and watched the miller grind the wheat into flour. When she finally came back, the Little Red Hen said to the others, "Who will help me mix this flour into dough, so that I can bake some bread?"

"Not I," growled the Dog.

"Not I," meowed the Cat.

"Not I," grunted the Pig.

"Then I will mix the dough and bake the bread all by myself," clucked the Little Red Hen.

When the bread was baked, a delicious smell filled the barnyard. The animals gathered around the Little Red Hen. "Who will help me eat this bread?" she asked them.

"I will!" barked the Dog.

"I will!" purred the Cat.

"I will!" squealed the Pig.

"No, you won't," said the Little Red Hen, tying a napkin around her neck. "I planted the wheat by myself. I cut and threshed it. I took it to the mill. I mixed the dough and baked the bread all by myself. Now I will eat the bread—all by myself."

And that's just what she did!

The Three Little Pigs

There was once a mother pig who had three little pigs. When the little pigs were old enough, their mother sent them off to seek their fortunes.

The first little pig met a man with a bundle of straw. He said to the man, "Please, sir, give me some straw to build a house."

The man gave him some straw, and the little pig built a house with it. Soon a wolf came and knocked on the door.

"Little pig, little pig, let me come in," said the wolf.

But the pig answered, "No, not by the hair of my chinny-chin-chin."

And the wolf said, "Then I'll huff, and I'll puff, and I'll blow your house in." So he huffed . . . and he puffed . . . and he blew the house in. Then he gobbled up the first little pig.

The second little pig met a man with a bundle of sticks, and he said, "Please, sir, give me some sticks to build a house."

The man gave him some sticks, and the pig built a house with them. Then along came the very same wolf and said, "Little pig, little pig, let me come in."

"No, not by the hair of my chinny-chin-chin."

"Then I'll huff, and I'll puff, and I'll blow your house in," said the wolf. He huffed . . . and he puffed . . . and at last he blew the house in. Then he gobbled up the second little pig.

The third little pig met a man with a load of bricks, and he said, "Please, sir, give me some bricks to build a house."

So the man gave him some bricks, and the pig built a strong house for himself. Along came the wolf, saying, "Little pig, little pig, let me come in."

"No, not by the hair of my chinny-chin-chin," said the third little pig.

"Then I'll huff, and I'll puff, and I'll blow your house in," said the wolf.

Well, he huffed . . . and he puffed . . . and he puffed . . . and he huffed, but he could *not* blow the house in. He said slyly, "Little pig, I know where there is a nice field of turnips."

"Where?" asked the little pig.

"I'll be glad to show you tomorrow," said the wolf. "Be ready at six o'clock in the morning, and I will call for you. Then we will go pick turnips together."

"Very well," said the little pig.

But the little pig knew where the turnip field was, so he rose at five and went to get turnips by himself. When the wolf arrived at the little pig's house at six, the little pig was back safe at home.

The wolf was very angry when he learned that the little pig already had a potful of turnips for his dinner. Then he thought of a new trick.

"Little pig," said the wolf, "I know where there is a nice apple tree."

"Where?" said the pig.

"I will come for you at five o'clock tomorrow morning," said the wolf, "and show you where the apple tree is."

But the little pig knew exactly where the apple tree could be found, so he awakened at four o'clock the next morning and went off for apples. The wolf got up early, too, however, and arrived at the apple tree to find the pig up in the tree, still picking apples. Seeing the wolf, the little pig became very frightened.

The wolf called up to him, "Little pig! You *are* an early riser! Are the apples good?"

"Yes, very," said the little pig. "I will throw one down to you. You may judge for yourself."

But the pig threw the apple so far that the wolf had to run
and get it. The little pig had only enough time to jump down
from the tree and race home.

The next day the wolf came to the pig's house again.
"Little pig," he said, "the county fair begins this afternoon.
Will you go?"

"Oh, yes," said the pig. "What time shall I be ready?"

"At three," said the wolf.

So the little pig left his house long before three and got to
the fair and bought a butter churn. He was on his way home
when he saw the wolf coming up a hill toward him. The
little pig jumped into the churn to hide, but the churn fell
over and rolled down the hill. The strange object rolled
toward the wolf, frightening him so much that he ran home
without going to the fair.

Later he went to the little pig's house and told him about the big round thing that had come rolling down the hill. The little pig laughed and told the wolf about the butter churn he had bought at the fair.

The wolf had been tricked again! Now he was so angry that he climbed up to the roof of the little pig's house. From there he would slide down the chimney and gobble the pig at last.

When the little pig heard the wolf on the roof, he hung a pot of water in the fireplace and quickly lit a blazing fire. Just as the wolf came down the chimney, the little pig took the cover off the boiling pot. PLOP! The wolf dropped in.

That was the end of the wolf. This is the end of the story!

The City Mouse and the Country Mouse

There was once a mouse—a plain, sensible sort of mouse—who lived by himself far out in the country. One day a friend who lived in the city came to visit him. The Country Mouse served his friend a supper of freshly picked peas, golden corn, and a bit of cheddar cheese. The City Mouse only picked at what was served—a nibble here and a nibble there—wondering how his friend could enjoy such plain food.

After dinner the City Mouse said to the Country Mouse, "My good friend, how can you be happy here in the country? There is no fun here, no gaiety. Everything is dull and humdrum—even the food. Why don't you come with me to the city and see the exciting life that I lead?"

The Country Mouse agreed, and as soon as it was dark, they started off for the city. They arrived in time to learn that a splendid dinner was being given in the mansion where the City Mouse lived. When the guests left the dining room, the servants took the leftover food to the big pantry.

The two mice, who had been waiting in the pantry, began feasting as soon as the door was shut. There was juicy roast beef and delicious gravy, plump rolls and bowls of salad. The Country Mouse could hardly believe his eyes!

Suddenly the door opened, and a maid came into the pantry. The two mice hid behind the flour bin while she bustled about. When she was gone, the friends returned to their feast.

Once again the door opened, and a boy looking for a piece of cake rushed in, followed by his noisy dog.

The City Mouse ran to the safety of a mouse hole in the pantry wall, which, by the way, he had not been thoughtful enough to show to his friend. By the time the Country Mouse found the hole, he was trembling with fear and could scarcely calm down. When the City Mouse asked him if he wanted to continue their feast, the Country Mouse shook his tiny head. "Oh, no," he said. "Your exciting city life is too much for me. What I want is peace and quiet in the country."

And with that, the Country Mouse put on his cap, hurried out of the big house, and headed straight for home in the country.

Teeny-Tiny

Once upon a time there was a teeny-tiny woman who lived in a teeny-tiny house in a teeny-tiny village. Now, one day this teeny-tiny woman put on her teeny-tiny bonnet and went out of her teeny-tiny house to take a teeny-tiny walk.

When the teeny-tiny woman had gone a teeny-tiny way, she came to a teeny-tiny gate. The teeny-tiny woman opened the teeny-tiny gate and went into a teeny-tiny churchyard.

When the teeny-tiny woman was walking in the teeny-tiny churchyard, she happened to see a teeny-tiny bone lying on a teeny-tiny grave.

The teeny-tiny woman said to her teeny-tiny self, "This teeny-tiny bone will make me some teeny-tiny soup for my teeny-tiny supper." So the teeny-tiny woman put the teeny-tiny bone into her teeny-tiny pocket and went home to her teeny-tiny house.

The teeny-tiny woman was a teeny-tiny bit tired after her teeny-tiny walk, so she went to her teeny-tiny bedroom. She put the teeny-tiny bone into a teeny-tiny cupboard and lay down for a teeny-tiny nap.

When the teeny-tiny woman had been asleep a teeny-tiny time, she was awakened by a teeny-tiny voice calling from the teeny-tiny cupboard, which said:

"Give me my bone!"

The teeny-tiny woman was a teeny-tiny bit frightened, so she hid her teeny-tiny head further under the teeny-tiny covers. When she had been asleep again for only a teeny-tiny time, the teeny-tiny voice in the teeny-tiny cupboard cried out again, a teeny-tiny louder,

"GIVE ME MY BONE!"

This made the teeny-tiny woman a teeny-tiny bit more frightened, so she hid her teeny-tiny head a teeny-tiny bit further under the teeny-tiny covers. When the teeny-tiny woman had been asleep again for only a teeny-tiny time, the teeny-tiny voice from the teeny-tiny cupboard said again, a teeny-tiny louder,

"GIVE ME MY BONE!"

The teeny-tiny woman was a teeny-tiny bit more frightened, but she pulled her teeny-tiny head out from under the teeny-tiny covers and said in her loudest teeny-tiny voice,

"TAKE IT!"

The Elves and the Shoemaker

There was once an honest shoemaker who worked hard but could not seem to earn his living. Things grew worse until, at last, all he had left was enough leather to make one more pair of shoes.

That night he cut the leather so that he could sew the shoes together the next day. Then he and his good wife went off to bed and fell asleep.

In the morning the shoemaker sat down to work, when, to his astonishment, he saw a newly made pair of shoes upon the table! He looked them over carefully. There was not one false stitch in the whole job. The shoes were lovely.

That day a customer came in and willingly paid a high price for the well-made shoes. The grateful shoemaker bought enough leather with the money to make two more pairs of shoes.

In the evening the shoemaker cut the leather and went to bed early so that he might get up and stitch the shoes the next day. But he was saved the trouble, because when he got up in the morning, the work was already finished.

Customers paid him well for his goods that day—so well that he bought enough leather to make four more pairs of shoes. Again he began the work at night and found it finished the morning after.

39

And so it went for some time. What was set out in the
evening was always done by daybreak, and the shoemaker
and his wife were no longer poor.

One evening before Christmas, as the shoemaker and his
wife sat in front of the fire together, he said to her, "I would
like to stay up tonight to see who it is that comes and does
my work for me." His wife agreed, so they left a light
burning in the room and hid behind a curtain to watch what
might happen.

As soon as it was midnight, two frisky little elves who
wore no clothes came dancing in the door. They sat upon the
shoemaker's bench and took up all the work that was laid
out. Their little fingers began to stitch and rap and tap so
quickly that the shoemaker and his wife were amazed.

The next day the wife said to the shoemaker, "Those little elves have nothing on their backs to keep off the cold. I must make them each a shirt, a coat, and a pair of trousers. And you must make them two pairs of tiny shoes."

The shoemaker happily agreed. Soon the clothes and shoes were ready and put out in a row on the shoemaker's bench.

That night the shoemaker and his wife hid themselves again to see what the little elves would do.

At midnight the elves came in. They sat down to work as usual. Suddenly they saw the clothes on the table and began to laugh and smile with delight. They dressed themselves in the twinkling of an eye and danced about as merry as could be. At last they danced out the door and into the night.

From that time on, everything went well for the shoemaker and his wife, and they lived happily, although they never saw the elves again.

The Milkmaid

One day a milkmaid walked down the road on her way to market. She balanced a milk pitcher on her head and thought about the money she would get from selling the milk.

"I shall have enough to buy four chickens!" she said to herself.

Then she thought some more. "The chickens will lay a hundred eggs. The eggs will hatch. I will sell all the chickens, and then I will have enough money to buy a pig!"

The milkmaid went on walking and thinking. "The pig will grow big and fat. I will sell the big, fat pig, and then I will have enough money to buy a cow and a sweet baby calf!"

The thought of it made the milkmaid so happy that she forgot the pitcher on her head and began to skip. The pitcher fell to the ground and broke, and the milk spilled onto the road.

When the poor milkmaid got home, she told her father what had happened.

Her father shook his head. "Next time, daughter," he said, "don't count your chickens before they hatch."

The Hare and the Tortoise

"What a slow fellow you are!" said a Hare to a Tortoise one day. "I pity anyone who must creep along as you do!"

"Really?" said the Tortoise. "Suppose we run a race. Slow as I am, I will beat you."

"What a boaster you are!" said the Hare. "Everyone knows I am the fastest runner in the field."

"Let's ask the Fox to mark the course and be the judge," said the Tortoise.

"Very well," said the Hare, but he laughed at the thought of such a race.

The Fox showed them how far they had to run. Then he gave a sharp, foxy bark, and the race was on.

The Tortoise plodded forward at his usual unhurried pace. The Hare leaped past the Tortoise and soon left him far behind. Then he stopped to wait for the Tortoise. The sun was hot, and the Hare grew sleepy. He lay down in the shade by the side of the road and had a pleasant nap.

When the Hare woke up at last, he did not know how much time had passed. He ran as fast as he could, but when he came to the end of the course, he saw the Tortoise slowly crossing the finish line.

No longer boastful, the Hare crept away while the judge gave a prize to the happy Tortoise.

The House That Jack Built

This is the House that Jack built.

This is the Malt that lay in the House that Jack built.

This is the Rat
that ate the Malt,
that lay in the House
that Jack built.

This is the Cat
that killed the Rat,
that ate the Malt,
that lay in the House
that Jack built.

This is the Dog
that worried the Cat,
that killed the Rat,
that ate the Malt,
that lay in the House
that Jack built.

49

This is the Cow
with the crumpled horn
that tossed the Dog,
that worried the Cat,
that killed the Rat,
that ate the Malt,
that lay in the House
that Jack built.

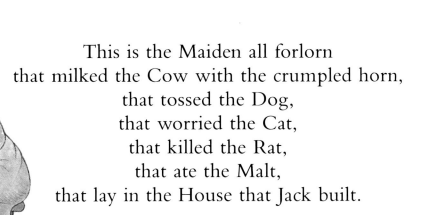

This is the Maiden all forlorn
that milked the Cow with the crumpled horn,
that tossed the Dog,
that worried the Cat,
that killed the Rat,
that ate the Malt,
that lay in the House that Jack built.

This is the Man all tattered and torn
that kissed the Maiden all forlorn,
that milked the Cow with the crumpled horn,
that tossed the Dog,
that worried the Cat,
that killed the Rat,
that ate the Malt,
that lay in the House that Jack built.

This is the Priest all shaven and shorn
that married the Man all tattered and torn,
that kissed the Maiden all forlorn,
that milked the Cow with the crumpled horn,
that tossed the Dog,
that worried the Cat,
that killed the Rat,
that ate the Malt,
that lay in the House that Jack built.

This is the Cock that crowed in the morn
that waked the Priest all shaven and shorn,
that married the Man all tattered and torn,
that kissed the Maiden all forlorn,
that milked the Cow with the crumpled horn,
that tossed the Dog,
that worried the Cat,
that killed the Rat,
that ate the Malt,
that lay in the House that Jack built.

This is the Farmer who sowed the corn
that fed the Cock that crowed in the morn,
that waked the Priest all shaven and shorn,
that married the Man all tattered and torn,
that kissed the Maiden all forlorn,
that milked the Cow with the crumpled horn,
that tossed the Dog,
that worried the Cat,
that killed the Rat,
that ate the Malt,
that lay in the House that Jack built.

The Owl and the Pussycat

The Owl and the Pussycat went to sea
    In a beautiful pea-green boat,
They took some honey, and plenty of money,
    Wrapped up in a five-pound note.
The Owl looked up to the stars above,
    And sang to a small guitar,
"O lovely Pussy! O Pussy, my love,
    What a beautiful Pussy you are,
            You are,
            You are!
    What a beautiful Pussy you are!"

Pussy said to the Owl, "You elegant fowl!
 How charmingly sweet you sing!
O let us be married! Too long we have tarried:
 But what shall we do for a ring?"
They sailed away, for a year and a day,
 To the land where the Bong-tree grows;
And there in a wood a Piggy-wig stood,
 With a ring at the end of his nose,
  His nose,
  His nose,
 With a ring at the end of his nose.

"Dear Pig, are you willing to sell for one shilling
   Your ring?" Said the Piggy, "I will."
So they took it away, and were married next day
   By the Turkey who lives on the hill.
They dined on mince, and slices of quince,
   Which they ate with a runcible spoon;
And hand in hand, on the edge of the sand,
   They danced by the light of the moon,
         The moon,
         The moon,
   They danced by the light of the moon.

—*Edward Lear*

The Duel

The gingham dog and the calico cat
Side by side on the table sat;
'Twas half-past twelve, and (what do you think!)
Nor one nor t'other had slept a wink!
　　The old Dutch clock and the Chinese plate
　　Appeared to know as sure as fate
There was going to be a terrible spat.
　　(I wasn't there; I simply state
　　What was told to me by the Chinese plate!)

The gingham dog went, "Bow-wow-wow!"
And the calico cat replied, "Mee-ow!"
The air was littered, an hour or so,
With bits of gingham and calico,
　　While the old Dutch clock in the chimney-place
　　Up with its hands before its face,
For it always dreaded a family row!
　　(Now mind: I'm only telling you
　　What the old Dutch clock declares is true!)

The Chinese plate looked very blue,
And wailed, "Oh, dear! What shall we do!"
But the gingham dog and the calico cat
Wallowed this way and tumbled that,
    Employing every tooth and claw,
    In the awfullest way you ever saw—
And, oh! How the gingham and calico flew!
    (Don't fancy I exaggerate—
    I got my news from the Chinese plate!)

Next morning, where the two had sat,
They found no trace of dog or cat;
And some folks think unto this day
That burglars stole that pair away!
　　But the truth about the cat and pup
　　Is this: they ate each other up!
Now what do you really think of that!
　　(The old Dutch clock it told me so,
　　And that is how I came to know.)

—*Eugene Field*

Button Soup

Once there was an old woman who had little money but was blessed with a great deal of cleverness. One day the old woman decided to leave her home and go visit her daughter, who lived far away.

At the end of the first day she was hungry and tired. As she came to a small village, she knocked on the door of the first house. A little old man who was a dreadful miser opened the door just a crack and peeked out.

"Excuse me," said the old woman, "but I am hungry and tired from my travels. Would you have a bit of food for me?"

The little old man shouted through the crack in the door, "No, I have no food to give you. I barely have enough food for myself!"

"Oh, dear. I see," said the old woman. "Then perhaps you could spare a bed for me to sleep in? I would be very grateful."

"A bed?" said the little old man. "Well, maybe I could spare a bed. But you will have to promise not to make any trouble of any kind."

The little old man opened the door and led the woman into the kitchen. "You can sleep there," he said, pointing to a narrow cot next to the stove. "And remember, no trouble!"

"No, not a bit," said the old woman. "But I wonder if I could have a drink of water. If you will be so kind, then I will show you how to make soup with a button."

"Soup with a button?" said the little old man. "Ridiculous!"

But the stingy fellow was curious in spite of himself. "If I could make soup with a button," he said, "I would never go hungry." He gave the woman a drink of water. Then he brought a potful of water and set it on the stove so that she could make the soup.

The old woman pulled a button from her pocket and dropped it into the pot. "There," she said. "The first thing you need for button soup is a button. But button soup wouldn't be very tasty without salt. Do you happen to have a little salt?"

The little old man grumbled, but he opened the cupboard door and took out some salt. As he did so, the old woman noticed some onions and potatoes in the cupboard. She said nothing as she stirred the salt into the water.

After a while, the old woman said, "Oh, this soup would be especially fine if only we had an onion and some potatoes."

The little old man grumbled, but he looked for an onion and some potatoes and handed them to the old woman. When they were simmering in the pot and the soup was beginning to smell delicious, the old woman said, "Oh, the soup would be absolutely unforgettable if only we had some carrots and meat."

This time the little old man did not even bother to grumble. The good smell of the soup had made the miser very hungry. He quickly went and found carrots and some meat, and the old woman put them into the pot. Then the two of them sat down and waited while the soup simmered.

When it was nearly ready, the old woman said, "I know that I promised not to make any trouble, and I know that you have no food in the house, but this fine soup really should be eaten with a little bread and a little wine."

"True, true," said the little old man. "The soup is such a simple dish, surely we can allow ourselves a bit of bread and wine to go with it."

In the end, the little old man and the old woman ate large bowls of soup and shared a good loaf of bread and a fine bottle of wine and enjoyed themselves enormously.

That night, the old woman slept on the cot next to the stove. The next morning, before continuing her journey, she thanked the little old man for all the trouble he had gone to.

"Oh, no trouble at all," said the little old man. "After all, it was you who went to the bother of showing me how to make fine soup with just a tiny button."

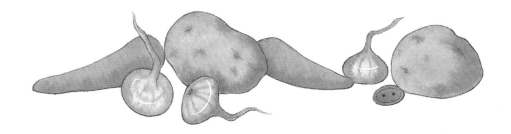

The Little Engine That Could™

Chug, chug, chug. *Puff, puff, puff. Ding-dong, ding-dong.* The little train rumbled over the tracks. She was a happy little train, for she had a jolly load to carry. Her cars were filled with toy animals, all kinds of dolls, and the funniest little toy clown you ever saw.

Some of the cars were filled with good things for children to eat—big golden oranges, red-cheeked apples, peppermint drops, and lollipops. The little train was carrying these wonderful things to the good boys and girls on the other side of the mountain.

The little train's engine puffed along merrily. Then all of a sudden she stopped with a jerk. She simply could not go another inch. Oh, dear! What were the dolls and animals to do?

"Here comes a shiny new engine," said the little toy clown, waving a red flag. "Let us ask him to help us."

So all the dolls and toys cried out together, "Please, Shiny New Engine, won't you pull our little train over the mountain? Our engine has broken down!"

But the Shiny New Engine snorted, "I pull you? I am a Passenger Engine. I have just carried a fine big train with sleeping cars and a dining car over the mountain. I pull the likes of you? Indeed not!" And off he steamed to the roundhouse, where engines live when they are not busy.

How sad the little train and all the dolls and toys felt!

Then the little clown said to the others, "The Passenger Engine is not the only one in the world. Here comes another engine, a great big strong one. Let us ask him to help us."

The little toy clown waved his flag, and the big strong engine came to a stop.

"Please, oh please, Big Engine," cried all the dolls and toys. "Won't you pull our little train over the mountain?"

But the Big Strong Engine bellowed, "I am a Freight Engine. I have just pulled a long train loaded with heavy machines over the mountain. The machines will print books and newspapers for grown-ups to read. I am a very important engine, indeed. I won't pull the likes of you!" And the Freight Engine puffed off indignantly to the roundhouse.

The little train was very, very sad, and the dolls and toys were ready to cry.

"Cheer up," cried the little clown. "The Freight Engine is not the only one in the world. Here comes another. A little blue engine, a very little one. Maybe she will help us."

The very little engine came chug-chugging merrily along. When she saw the toy clown's flag, she stopped quickly.

"What is the matter, my friends?" she asked kindly.

"Oh, Little Blue Engine," cried the dolls and toys. "We have broken down. Please, please, will you pull us over the mountain?"

"I'm not very big," said the Little Blue Engine. "They only use me for switching trains in the yard. I have never even been over the mountain."

"The children on the other side won't have any toys to play with or good food to eat unless you help us, Little Blue Engine," said all the dolls and toys.

The very little engine looked up and saw tears in the dolls' eyes. She thought about the children waiting on the other side of the mountain.

Then she said, "I think I can. I think I can. I think I can."
And she hitched herself to the little train.

She tugged and pulled, and pulled and tugged, and slowly,
slowly, slowly they started off.

The dolls and toy animals smiled and began to cheer.

Puff, puff, chug, chug, went the Little Blue Engine. "I think
I can—I think I can—I think I can."

Up, up, up. The little engine climbed and climbed—until
at last they reached the top of the mountain.

"Hurray! Hurray!" cried the clown and all the dolls and toys. "The boys and girls will be happy now—because you helped us, Little Blue Engine."

The Little Blue Engine smiled. She seemed to say, as she puffed steadily down the mountain:

"I thought I could.

    I thought I could.

        I thought I could.

            I thought I could."

—*Watty Piper*

The Velveteen Rabbit

or How Toys Become Real

(Abridged from the original story by Margery Williams.)

There was once a velveteen rabbit, and in the beginning he was really splendid. His soft coat was spotted brown and white, and his ears were lined with pink sateen. On Christmas morning, when he sat wedged in the top of the Boy's stocking, the effect was charming.

For at least two hours the Boy loved him, and then, in the excitement of looking at all the new presents, the Velveteen Rabbit was forgotten.

For a long time he lived in the toy cupboard, and no one thought very much about him. He was naturally shy, and some of the expensive mechanical toys snubbed him. The only person who was kind to him at all was the Skin Horse.

The Skin Horse had lived longer in the nursery than any of the others. He was wise, for he had seen many mechanical toys arrive and pass away, and he knew that they were only toys and would never turn into anything else.

"What is REAL?" asked the Rabbit one day. "Does it mean having things that buzz inside you and a stick-out handle?"

"Real isn't how you are made," said the Skin Horse. "It's a thing that happens to you. When a child really loves you for a long, long time, you become Real. It doesn't happen all at once. Generally, by the time you are Real, most of your hair has been loved off, and you get very shabby."

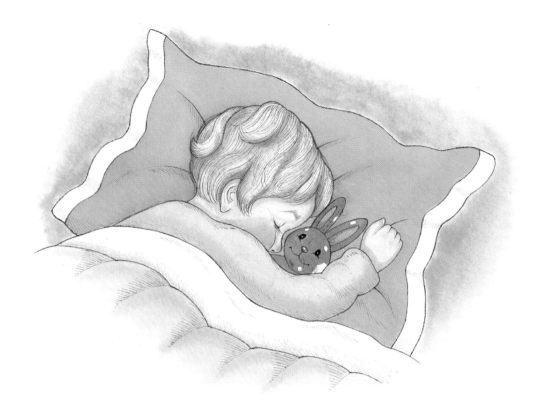

The Rabbit sighed. He longed to become Real, to know what it felt like, even if it meant becoming shabby.

One evening, when the Boy was going to bed, Nana reached into the toy cupboard and gave him the Rabbit to sleep with. That night, and for many nights after, the Velveteen Rabbit slept with the Boy. At first he found it rather uncomfortable, for the Boy hugged him tight. But very soon he grew to like it, for the Boy talked to him and made nice tunnels for him under the bedclothes that he said were like the burrows that real rabbits lived in.

And so time went on, and the little Rabbit was very happy—so happy that he never noticed how his beautiful velveteen fur was getting shabbier and shabbier, and how all the pink had rubbed off his nose where the Boy had kissed him.

Spring came, and summer, and they had long days in the garden, for wherever the Boy went, the Rabbit went too. He had rides in the wheelbarrow, and picnics on the grass, and lovely fairy huts built for him under the raspberry canes behind the flower border.

Then came the finest day of all—when the Boy told Nana that his Rabbit wasn't a toy at all, that he was Real. When the Rabbit heard what the Boy had said, so much love stirred in his little sawdust heart that it almost burst.

And then, one day, the Boy was ill. His face grew very flushed, and he talked in his sleep, and his little body was so hot that it burned the Rabbit when the Boy held him close.

When, at last, the Boy got well, the doctor ordered that all the books and toys that the Boy had played with in bed must be burned.

"His old bunny, too," the doctor said. "It's a mass of scarlet fever germs! Get rid of it at once."

And so the little Rabbit was put into a sack and carried out to the end of the garden.

That night the Boy had a new bunny to sleep with him. While the Boy was asleep in the house, the little Rabbit lay in a corner of the garden. By wriggling a bit the Rabbit was able to get his head through the opening of the sack and look out.

He thought of those long sunlit hours in the garden—
how happy they were—and a great sadness came over him.
Of what use was it to be loved and lose one's beauty and
become Real if it all ended like this? And a tear, a real tear,
trickled down his shabby velvet nose and fell to the ground.

And then a strange thing happened. For where the tear
had fallen, a beautiful flower grew out of the ground.
Presently the blossom opened into a golden cup, and out of it
stepped a lovely fairy. She kissed the little Rabbit on his
velveteen nose that was all damp from crying.

"I am the nursery magic Fairy," she said. "I take care of all the playthings that the children have loved. When they are old and worn out, I come and take them away with me and turn them into Real."

"Wasn't I Real before?" asked the little Rabbit.

"You were Real to the Boy," the Fairy said, "because he loved you. Now you shall be Real to everyone." And she held the little Rabbit close in her arms and flew with him into the moonlit wood where the wild rabbits danced. The fairy kissed the little Rabbit again and put him down on the grass.

"Run and play, little Rabbit!" she said.

And he found that he actually could hop about! Instead of dingy velveteen, he had soft, shiny brown fur, and his ears twitched by themselves.

He was a Real Rabbit at last, at home with the other rabbits.

Autumn and winter passed, and in the spring, the Boy went out to play in the wood. And while he was playing, a rabbit crept out from the bracken and peeped at him.

"Why, he looks just like my old Bunny that was lost when I had scarlet fever!" the Boy thought to himself.

But he never knew that it really *was* his own Bunny, come back to look at the child who had first helped him to be Real.

The Ugly Duckling

It was summertime in the country. The sun shone brightly on the farmland and on the green meadows dotted with wildflowers. A gentle breeze rustled the leaves in the trees.

Near a large stone house and a pond, a duck sat patiently on a nest she had made for herself. Now and then she wished that a visitor might come by to keep her company. But no one did.

Crack! Suddenly one of the eggs in the nest that the duck had been keeping warm opened up—and out tumbled a fuzzy duckling!

Crack! Crack! More eggs cracked open, each one hatching another fuzzy duckling. But the last duckling looked much different from the others. "Can he possibly be a turkey chick?" the mother duck asked herself. "I have heard that turkeys hate the water, so we shall soon find out."

The next day the mother duck led her new family through the cattails to the cool water of the pond.

Splash! Into the water the mother duck sprang, sending ripples among the lily pads. "Quack, quack!" she said, and one after another her ducklings plopped in after her. They all seemed to know how to swim, even the ugly gray one.

"No, that is no turkey," the mother duck said to herself. "See how beautifully he uses his legs, how straight he holds his neck. He must surely be my own duckling."

After their swim, the ducklings followed the mother duck to the farmyard next to the large stone house. There were many other ducks there, as well as hens, roosters and geese. All of the ducklings were made to feel welcome—except the one who seemed so ugly. He was pushed around and teased by the others. The hens pecked at him. The geese beat their wings at him, and the larger ducks chased him to every corner of the yard.

The mother duck tried her best to protect her duckling, but she could not stop the farmyard animals from nipping at him and chasing him. And so, one day in early autumn, the ugly duckling ran away to a marshland where there was no one to bother him.

The cold winter months that followed were cruel to the poor ugly duckling. Though he was neither bitten nor chased, he often could not find enough to eat. At night he could only huddle under frozen grasses.

In time, however, warmer days told the duckling that spring had come. He raised his wings and they flapped strongly. Up, up in the air he rose, and soon he found himself flying over a beautiful pond in a large garden. As he drifted down he could see apple trees and lilacs in bloom.

No sooner had he settled himself than he saw three beautiful white birds swimming toward him. How elegant they were!

But the joy at seeing these magnificent birds soon gave way to sadness. "What must they think of me and my ugliness?" he thought. "They'll only want to peck me to bits because I am so ugly." He remembered the teasing and chases around the farmyard and the hunger he had felt during the long, cold winter. "Perhaps it is just as well that my life should end here and now, among all this beauty," he thought to himself.

Bravely the ugly duckling swam to meet the magnificent white swans, for that is what they were. When the swans saw him coming, they darted toward him with ruffled feathers.

The duckling stopped in the water, his head bowed, awaiting the swans' attack. But as he waited, he saw his reflection in the water below.

It had been a long time since he had seen his reflection. And what a surprise he found! Instead of an ugly, clumsy creature, he saw the image of a long-necked white bird that looked just like the approaching swans. He too was a swan!

The other swans now swam around him and stroked him with friendly bills. Some children came to the edge of the pond with corn and pieces of bread to throw in the water. When they saw the new swan in the pond, they said that he was the prettiest of all, since he was so young and handsome.

The new swan felt a little strange, being called pretty. He hid his head under his wing shyly.

But as the sweet smell of lilacs filled the air and the bright sun peeked out from behind a cloud, the swan knew that he was where he belonged. He rustled his feathers and raised his slender neck high, feeling both happy and proud.

The Night Before Christmas

'Twas the night before Christmas
    when all through the house,
Not a creature was stirring, not even a mouse.

The stockings were hung by the chimney with care,
In hopes that St. Nicholas soon would be there.

The children were nestled all snug in their beds,
While visions of sugarplums danced in their heads.

Mama in her kerchief and I in my cap
Had just settled down for a long winter's nap,

When out on the lawn there arose such a clatter,
I sprang from my bed to see what was the matter.

Away to the window I flew like a flash,
Tore open the shutters and threw up the sash.

The moon on the breast of the new-fallen snow
Gave a luster of midday to objects below,

When, what to my wondering eyes should appear,
But a miniature sleigh and eight tiny reindeer,

With a little old driver so lively and quick,
I knew in a moment it must be St. Nick!

More rapid than eagles his coursers they came,
And he whistled and shouted and called them by name:

"Now, Dasher! Now, Dancer! Now, Prancer and Vixen!
On, Comet! On, Cupid! On, Donder and Blitzen!

To the top of the porch! To the top of the wall!
Now, dash away! Dash away! Dash away all!"

As dry leaves that before the wild hurricane fly,
When they meet with an obstacle, mount to the sky,

So up to the housetop the coursers they flew,
With a sleigh full of toys, and St. Nicholas, too.

And then in a twinkling I heard on the roof
The prancing and pawing of each little hoof.

As I drew in my head and was turning around,
Down the chimney St. Nicholas came with a bound.

He was dressed all in fur from his head to his foot,
And his clothes were all tarnished with ashes and soot.

A bundle of toys he had flung on his back,
And he looked like a peddler just opening his pack.

His eyes, how they twinkled! His dimples, how merry!
His cheeks were like roses, his nose like a cherry!

His droll little mouth was drawn up like a bow,
And the beard on his chin was as white as the snow.

The stump of a pipe he held tight in his teeth,
And the smoke it encircled his head like a wreath.

He had a broad face and a little round belly
That shook when he laughed like a bowl full of jelly.

He was chubby and plump, a right jolly old elf,
And I laughed when I saw him, in spite of myself.

A wink of his eye and a twist of his head
Soon gave me to know I had nothing to dread.

He spoke not a word, but went straight to his work,
And filled all the stockings, then turned with a jerk,

And laying his finger aside of his nose,
And giving a nod, up the chimney he rose.

He sprang to his sleigh, to his team gave a whistle,
And away they all flew like the down of a thistle.

But I heard him exclaim ere he drove out of sight:

"HAPPY CHRISTMAS TO ALL,
AND TO ALL A GOOD NIGHT!"

—*Clement C. Moore*